OLD MOTHER HUBBARD

AND HER WONDERFUL DOG

ILLUSTRATED BY

JAMES MARSHALL

M
PAN MACMILLAN CHILDREN'S BOOKS

First published 1991 by Harper Collins Canada Ltd

This Picturemac edition published 1994 by Pan Macmillan Children's Books
a division of Pan Macmillan Publishers Limited
Cavaye Place London SW10 9PG
and Basingstoke

Associated companies throughout the world

ISBN 0 333 60544 6

1 3 5 7 9 8 6 4 2

A CIP catalogue for this book is available from
the British Library

Printed in Hong Kong

Old Mother Hubbard
Went to the cupboard,
To fetch her poor dog a bone;

But when she came there
The cupboard was bare
And so the poor dog had none.

She went to the baker
To buy him some bread;

But when she came back
The poor dog was dead.

She went to the undertaker
To buy him a coffin;

But when she came back
The poor dog was laughing.

She took a clean dish
To get him some tripe;

But when she came back
He was smoking a pipe.

She went to the fishmonger
To buy him some fish;

But when she came back
He was licking his dish.

She went to the tavern
For white wine and red;

But when she came back
The dog stood on his head.

She went to the fruit stand
To buy him some fruit;

But when she came back
He was playing the flute.

She went to the tailor
To buy him a coat;

But when she came back
He was riding a goat.
WE DO AMUSE OURSELVES

She went to the hatter
To buy him a hat;

But when she got back
He was feeding the cat.

She went to the barber
To buy him a wig;

But when she came back
He was dancing a jig.

She went to the cobbler
To buy him some shoes;

But when she came back
He was reading the news.

She went to the seamstress
To buy him some linen;

But when she came back
The dog was a-spinning.

She went to the hosier
To buy him some hose;

But when she came back

He was dressed in his clothes.
The dame made a curtsey,
The dog made a bow;

The dame said, Your servant,
The dog said:

Other Picturemacs you will enjoy

THE HOUSE THAT JACK BUILT Emily Bolam
GUMBOOT'S CHOCOLATEY DAY Mick Inkpen
JAKE AND THE BABYSITTER Simon James
HERDS OF WORDS Patricia MacCarthy
ALISTAIR'S ELEPHANT Marilyn Sadler/Roger Bollen
MY GRAMPA'S GOT BIG POCKETS Selina Young

For a complete list of Picturemac titles write to

Pan Macmillan Children's Books
Cavaye Place London SW10 9PG